The Cursed Necklace

Amy

DEDICATION

To all the silent guardians whose stories are buried in time, and to those who seek the truth behind every legend. This journey would not have been possible without the courage and wisdom of those who came before us.

I extend my deepest gratitude to the villagers who shared their memories, the elders who recounted their tales, and the historians who preserved our past. Your voices have breathed life into this narrative and have guided me through the shadows of our history.

Special thanks to Pandit Ravi Shankar for his unwavering support and insight, and to my friends and family who encouraged me every step of the way. Your belief in this project kept me going through the darkest nights.

To my readers, may you find as much inspiration and hope in these pages as I did in writing them. Let this story remind us all that understanding and compassion are the keys to unlocking the true power of our heritage.

ACKNOWLEDGMENTS

For Nani, who showed me the strength of family and the power of untold stories. Your wisdom and bravery have been my guiding light. Your love has been my anchor.

And for the spirit who taught us that understanding is the first step to healing. Your story deserved to be told, and your sacrifices should never be forgotten.

To the countless unseen protectors who guard us in silence and shadows, this is for you. And to every misunderstood soul, may this book be a beacon that brings light to your truth.

1 Echoes of the Past

Asha's weathered hands trembled as she brushed away the last clumps of damp soil. The late afternoon sun cast long shadows across her small garden, but it was the glint of metal that caught her eye. She leaned closer, her breath catching in her throat.

"What in the world?" she murmured, carefully extracting the object from its earthy tomb.

A necklace emerged, its intricate design dulled by years of burial but still unmistakably beautiful. Delicate silver chains intertwined, supporting a pendant adorned with swirling patterns and what appeared to be ancient symbols. As Asha held it up to the fading light, a chill ran down her spine despite the lingering heat of the day.

Something about this necklace felt... wrong. Asha couldn't shake the sensation that she had disturbed something best left hidden. But curiosity won out over caution. After all, she reasoned, it might be valuable. In a village where every rupee counted, such a find could make a real difference.

With a small grunt of effort, Asha pushed herself to her feet, wincing at the protests of her aging joints. She cast one last glance at the hole where the necklace had lain, then turned towards her modest home.

The moment Asha crossed the threshold, an eerie quiet descended. The usual chorus of evening birdsong abruptly ceased, leaving behind an unnatural stillness. She paused, frowning, but shook off the unsettling feeling. Probably just her imagination playing tricks.

As night fell, Asha settled into her favorite chair, examining the necklace more closely. Its weight felt oddly substantial in her palm, as if it carried more than just metal and gemstones. She traced a finger along the intricate patterns, marveling at the craftsmanship.

A sudden creaking sound from upstairs made her start. Asha's head snapped up, heart racing. "Hello?" she called out, her voice sounding small in the empty house. No response came, but the creaking continued, as if someone – or something – was pacing back and forth across the floor above.

Asha clutched the necklace tighter, her knuckles whitening. The house seemed to groan around her, timbers shifting and settling with alarming frequency. A chill draft whispered through the room, raising goosebumps on her arms despite the warm night.

"Stop it," Asha scolded herself. "You're an old woman letting your imagination run wild."

But even as she spoke the words aloud, trying to inject some normalcy into the oppressive silence, Asha couldn't shake the feeling that something had changed. Something dark and ancient had awoken, disturbed by her innocent discovery.

She stood, decision made. "I'll deal with this in the morning," Asha muttered, carefully placing the necklace on a high shelf. "Everything looks better in the light of day."

Sleep, however, proved elusive. Asha tossed and turned, plagued by half-formed nightmares and the persistent sensation of being watched. When she finally drifted off in the early hours of the morning, her dreams were filled with whispered warnings and shadowy figures just beyond her reach.

Dawn broke, painting the sky in hues of pink and gold. Asha rose, feeling every one of her years weighing heavily upon her. She shuffled to the kitchen, desperate for a cup of strong chai to clear the cobwebs from her mind.

As she waited for the water to boil, movement in the garden caught her eye. Asha peered out the window, squinting against the bright morning light. For a heart-stopping moment, she could have sworn she saw a figure standing among her carefully tended plants – a woman in flowing robes, her face obscured by shadow.

Asha blinked, and the apparition vanished. She shook her head, chiding herself for letting superstition get the better of her. Still, she couldn't quite shake the unease that had settled over her like a shroud.

With a steaming cup in hand, Asha made her way outside. The morning air was crisp, carrying the promise of another scorching day. She began her usual routine of watering the plants, trying to lose herself in the familiar task.

But as she worked, Asha couldn't help but notice how the shadows seemed to linger unnaturally, even as the sun climbed higher. They shifted and writhed at the corners of her vision, always retreating when she tried to focus on them directly.

A shiver ran through her, despite the growing heat. Asha straightened, wincing at the twinge in her back. She turned to head back inside, only to freeze in her tracks.

There, clearly visible in the full light of day, was a dark shape slithering across her porch. It moved with a fluid grace that defied natural explanation, undulating like smoke given form. Asha's breath caught in her throat, her heart pounding a frantic rhythm against her ribs.

The shadow paused, as if sensing her gaze. Slowly, it began to turn towards her. Asha stumbled backward, her watering can clattering to the ground. She squeezed her eyes shut, silently praying to any deity who might be listening.

When she dared to look again, the shadow was gone. But the feeling of wrongness lingered, as tangible as the sweat beading on her brow.

Asha hurried inside, her hands shaking as she bolted the door behind her. She leaned against it, trying to calm her racing heart. "This isn't right," she whispered to the empty house. "What have I unleashed?"

As if in answer, a gust of wind rattled the windows, carrying with it the faintest echo of laughter. Asha shuddered, her gaze drawn inexorably to the shelf where the necklace lay.

In the harsh light of day, its beauty seemed tarnished somehow. The intricate designs no longer appeared delicate and fascinating, but sinister – like a spider's web waiting to ensnare the unwary.

Asha's thoughts turned to her granddaughter, Priya, who was due to arrive that afternoon for a visit. A spark of hope ignited in her chest. Priya was young, educated in the ways of the modern world. Surely she would be able to make sense of these strange occurrences.

With renewed determination, Asha set about preparing for her granddaughter's arrival. She threw herself into cooking Priya's favorite dishes, hoping the familiar routines would drive away the lingering shadows.

But even as she worked, Asha couldn't shake the feeling that unseen eyes were watching her every move. The necklace seemed to pulse with an otherworldly energy, a silent promise of revelations yet to come.

Little did Asha know, her innocent discovery had set in motion a chain of events that would challenge everything she thought she knew about her family, her village, and the thin veil between this world and the next.

2 The Unsettling Welcome

The taxi jolts to a stop, kicking up a cloud of dust that swirls in the late afternoon sun. Priya leans forward, eager for her first glimpse of her grandmother's home. As the dust settles, her smile falters. Something feels... off.

"We're here, miss," the driver announces, catching her eye in the rearview mirror.

Priya nods, distracted. The usual warmth radiating from Asha's modest house seems muted somehow. Even the vibrant marigolds lining the path appear lackluster, their petals drooping in the heat.

She's barely taken two steps when Asha's voice rings out, tinged with an unfamiliar note of relief. "Priya! You're here!"

Her grandmother hurries down the path, arms outstretched. Priya embraces her, inhaling the familiar scent of sandalwood and spices. As she pulls back, her brow furrows. Dark circles shadow Asha's eyes, and fine lines of worry crease her forehead.

"Nani, is everything alright? You look tired," Priya says, studying her grandmother's face.

Asha waves away her concern with a forced laugh. "Oh, you know how it is at my age. Sleep doesn't come as easily as it used to." She ushers Priya inside, casting a wary glance over her shoulder before firmly shutting the door.

The interior of the house is cooler, but Priya can't shake the sensation of invisible cobwebs brushing against her skin. She suppresses a shiver.

"Come, come," Asha says, leading her to the kitchen. "I've made all your favorites. You must be hungry after your journey."

As they settle in with steaming plates of food, Priya observes her grandmother more closely. Asha's movements are jittery, her eyes darting to the shadows in the corners of the room.

"Nani," Priya begins carefully, "are you sure everything's okay? You seem... on edge."

Asha's smile falters for a moment before she rallies. "Of course, beta. I'm just excited to have you here." She hesitates, then adds, "Actually, there is something I want to show you. I found it in the garden yesterday."

Curiosity piqued, Priya follows Asha to the living room. Her grandmother reaches for a high shelf, retrieving a small cloth-wrapped bundle. With trembling hands, she unwraps it, revealing a stunning necklace.

Priya's eyes widen. "Oh, Nani, it's beautiful!" She leans closer, admiring the intricate metalwork and what appear to be ancient symbols etched into the pendant. "Where did you say you found this?"

"Buried in the backyard," Asha replies, her voice barely above a whisper. "I was gardening and... there it was."

Something in her grandmother's tone makes Priya look up sharply. Asha's face is pale, her eyes fixed on the necklace with a mixture of fascination and fear.

"Nani? What aren't you telling me?"

Asha sighs heavily, her shoulders slumping. "Ever since I found it, strange things have been happening. Noises in the night, shadows moving where they shouldn't... I know it sounds crazy, but–"

"It's okay," Priya says gently, taking her grandmother's hand. "I believe you. Why don't you tell me everything from the beginning?"

As Asha recounts the events of the past day, Priya listens intently. Part of her wants to dismiss it as the overactive imagination of an elderly woman living alone. But the genuine fear in Asha's eyes gives her pause.

"May I?" Priya asks, gesturing to the necklace. At Asha's nod, she carefully lifts it, surprised by its weight. The metal feels unnaturally cold against her skin, despite the warm evening.

Almost without thinking, Priya slips it over her head. The pendant settles against her chest, and for a moment, she could swear she feels a pulse of energy emanate from it.

"Oh, Priya, I don't know if you should–" Asha begins, but her words are cut off by a sudden gust of wind that sweeps through the room, rattling windows and extinguishing the lamps.

In the abrupt darkness, Priya feels a chill run down her spine. The necklace seems to grow heavier, pressing against her sternum like a physical manifestation of dread.

"Nani?" she calls out, her voice sounding small and frightened to her own ears.

"I'm here, beta," Asha replies, fumbling for matches. As the lamp flickers back to life, Priya gasps.

For a split second, she could have sworn she saw a figure standing in the corner of the room – a woman in flowing robes, her face obscured by shadow. But as quickly as it appeared, the apparition vanishes, leaving Priya to wonder if it had been a trick of the light.

"Did you see that?" she whispers, her heart racing.

Asha nods grimly. "Now do you understand why I've been so unsettled?"

Priya's scientific mind rebels against the idea of supernatural forces at work. There has to be a logical explanation. And yet... the weight of the necklace against her chest seems to whisper of ancient secrets and long-buried truths.

"We need help," Priya says decisively. "Is there someone in the village who might know more about this necklace? Its history?"

Asha's eyes light up. "The priest! Pandit Ravi has been here for decades. If anyone would know, it's him."

As night falls in earnest, Priya helps her grandmother prepare for bed. She can't help but notice how Asha triple-checks the locks, her gaze darting nervously to the windows.

"Try to get some rest, Nani," Priya says, kissing her cheek. "We'll go see the priest first thing in the morning."

But as Priya settles into her own bed, sleep proves elusive. The necklace lies on the nightstand, its intricate designs seeming to shift and change in the moonlight. She tosses and turns, her mind racing with questions.

When she finally drifts off, her dreams are vivid and terrifying. Priya finds herself running through darkened corridors, pursued by an unseen presence. Whispers echo in her ears, speaking in a language she can't understand but that fills her with an inexplicable dread.

A figure materializes before her – the same woman she thought she'd glimpsed earlier. But now Priya can see her face, contorted with rage and sorrow. The woman reaches out, her fingers like claws, and Priya screams–

She jolts awake, drenched in sweat and gasping for air. The necklace on the nightstand seems to pulse with an otherworldly light, keeping time with her racing heart.

Priya presses a hand to her chest, willing her breathing to slow. What had she and her grandmother stumbled into? And more importantly, how were they going to find their way out?

As the first hints of dawn creep through the window, Priya makes a silent vow. She will get to the bottom of this mystery, no matter what it takes. For her grandmother's sake, and for her own peace of mind.

Little does she know, the journey ahead will challenge everything she thought she knew about herself, her family, and the thin veil between this world and the next.

3 Echoes of Despair

Priya bolts upright in bed, a scream caught in her throat. Her heart pounds against her ribs as she gulps in air, trying to shake off the lingering tendrils of her nightmare. Sweat plasters her hair to her forehead, and her nightclothes cling uncomfortably to her skin.

"Not again," she whispers, her voice hoarse.

The room swims into focus as her eyes adjust to the darkness. For a moment, Priya swears she sees a figure lurking in the corner – a woman with long, flowing hair and eyes that glow with an otherworldly light. She blinks, and the apparition vanishes.

Priya fumbles for her phone, squinting at the harsh light of the screen. 3:17 AM. She's barely slept two hours.

With trembling hands, she reaches for the notebook on her bedside table. Priya's been documenting her dreams, hoping to make sense of the terrifying visions that plague her nights. She scribbles down what she can remember – the vengeful spirit, its face contorted with rage, reaching for her with clawed hands.

The details are sharper now, more vivid than ever before. Priya can almost feel the spirit's icy touch on her skin, smell the musty odor of decay that surrounds it. She shudders, setting the pen down.

"It's just a dream," Priya mutters, but the words ring hollow in the oppressive silence of the night.

She knows she won't be able to fall back asleep. Priya slips out of bed, wincing as her bare feet touch the cold floor. She pads quietly to the kitchen, not wanting to wake her grandmother.

As she waits for the kettle to boil, Priya catches a glimpse of her reflection in the window. She barely recognizes the gaunt face staring back at her. Dark circles rim her eyes, stark against her pale skin. Her cheekbones jut out sharply, testament to the weight she's lost in the past weeks.

The nightmares are taking their toll, and Priya knows it. She's irritable, jumping at every sudden noise. Concentrating on anything for more than a few minutes is a struggle. Even her passion for environmental activism has waned, her social media accounts lying dormant.

"Beta? What are you doing up at this hour?"

Priya startles at the sound of her grandmother's voice. Asha stands in the doorway, concern etched on her weathered face.

"Couldn't sleep," Priya says, forcing a smile. "Just making some tea. Want some?"

Asha nods, settling into a chair at the small kitchen table. She watches Priya with worried eyes as her granddaughter prepares two steaming cups of chai.

"The dreams again?" Asha asks softly as Priya sits across from her.

Priya nods, wrapping her hands around the warm mug. "They're getting worse, Nani. I can't... I can't shake them off anymore."

Asha reaches out, covering Priya's hand with her own. "We'll figure this out, beta. I promise."

But even as she speaks the words, Asha feels a flicker of doubt. She's never seen her vibrant, ambitious granddaughter look so defeated. The necklace's curse is sinking its claws deeper with each passing day, and Asha fears they're running out of time.

* * *

The next morning, Pandit Ravi Shankar arrives at Asha's home, his face grave. Priya barely looks up as he enters, slumped at the kitchen table with a mug of untouched coffee before her.

"Namaste, Panditji," Asha greets him, touching her palms together respectfully. "Thank you for coming."

The priest nods, his eyes flickering to Priya's huddled form. "The situation has escalated, hasn't it?"

Asha leads him to the living room, speaking in hushed tones. "The nightmares are worse than ever. Priya can barely eat or sleep. I'm at my wit's end, Panditji. What can we do?"

Pandit Ravi Shankar's brow furrows as he considers their options. After a long moment, he speaks. "There is a ritual – an ancient one – that might be able to break the curse. But it won't be easy."

Hope flares in Asha's chest. "Whatever it takes, we'll do it."

The priest nods solemnly. "We must act quickly. The ritual must be completed before the next full moon, when the curse's power will peak. If we fail..."

He doesn't need to finish the sentence. The consequences hang heavy in the air between them.

"What do we need to do?" Asha asks, steeling herself for whatever challenges lie ahead.

Pandit Ravi Shankar begins to explain the intricacies of the ritual, detailing the rare herbs and sacred items they'll need to gather. As he speaks, Priya appears in the doorway, drawn by the urgency in their voices.

"I want to help," she says, her voice hoarse but determined. "Whatever this ritual is, I need to be part of it."

Asha opens her mouth to protest, worried about putting more strain on her granddaughter. But the fire in Priya's eyes – a glimpse of her old self shining through – makes her pause.

"Of course, beta," Asha says instead. "We'll face this together."

* * *

The quest for the ritual components takes them to hidden corners of the village Priya never knew existed. Despite her weakened state, she insists on accompanying Asha and Pandit Ravi Shankar on their search.

They trek through overgrown paths to gather rare herbs that grow only in the shadow of an ancient banyan tree. Priya's botanist training comes in handy as she carefully identifies and harvests the delicate plants.

In a cave high in the nearby hills, they collect water from a sacred spring, said to have healing properties. The journey is arduous, and Priya has to stop frequently to catch her breath. But with each step, she feels a growing sense of purpose, a determination to see this through.

Their final stop is the village temple, where Pandit Ravi Shankar retrieves a set of blessed prayer beads, passed down through generations of priests. As he places them reverently in a silk pouch, Priya feels a ripple of energy in the air – a reminder of the powerful forces they're dealing with.

As they make their way back to Asha's home, the sun beginning to set, an uneasy feeling settles over Priya. The shadows seem to stretch longer than they should, and she can't shake the sensation of being watched.

"Nani," she whispers, gripping Asha's arm. "Do you feel that?"

Asha nods, her eyes darting around warily. "Let's hurry home, beta. We shouldn't be out after dark."

They quicken their pace, the gathered components clutched tightly to their chests. As they round the corner to Asha's street, a heart-wrenching howl splits the air.

"Raja!" Priya gasps, recognizing the cry of their family dog.

She breaks into a run, ignoring Asha's calls to wait. Priya bursts through the garden gate, her eyes scanning frantically for the loyal companion who's been part of their family for years.

A flash of golden fur catches her eye, and Priya's heart sinks. Raja lies motionless beneath the mango tree, his favorite spot in the garden.

"No, no, no," Priya murmurs, falling to her knees beside the dog. She reaches out with trembling hands, but recoils as she touches his cold, stiff body.

Asha and Pandit Ravi Shankar catch up, their faces falling as they take in the scene.

"What happened to him?" Priya asks, her voice cracking. "He was fine this morning!"

Asha kneels beside her granddaughter, placing a comforting hand on her shoulder. "I don't know, beta. But... I fear this may be another sign of the curse's power growing."

Priya turns to Pandit Ravi Shankar, anger flashing in her eyes. "Is this true? Is the curse killing innocent animals now?"

The priest's face is grim as he nods. "It's possible. As the curse's influence spreads, it may affect all living things in its path."

Priya's shoulders slump, the weight of their situation pressing down on her. Raja had been a constant presence in her visits to the village, his wagging tail and sloppy kisses always there to greet her. Now, he's another victim of this malevolent force they've unwittingly unleashed.

"We need to stop this," Priya says, her voice low and determined. "Whatever it takes, we have to break this curse before anyone else gets hurt."

As if in response to her words, a chill wind whips through the garden, rattling the leaves of the mango tree. For a moment, Priya swears she sees a shadowy figure standing at the edge of the property, watching them with glowing eyes.

She blinks, and it's gone. But the sense of urgency remains, a ticking clock counting down to the full moon – and their last chance to put things right.

* * *

That night, as Asha prepares for bed, a movement in her peripheral vision makes her freeze. She turns slowly, her heart pounding, to face the mirror above her dresser.

At first, she sees only her own reflection – an elderly woman with silver hair and worried eyes. But then, the image shifts. A younger woman appears behind her, dressed in flowing robes that seem to move of their own accord. The apparition's eyes burn with an otherworldly light, and its mouth opens in a silent scream.

Asha stumbles backward, her hand flying to her chest. "Who are you?" she whispers, her voice trembling. "What do you want from us?"

The ghostly figure raises a hand, pointing accusingly at Asha. Its lips move, but no sound emerges. As Asha watches, transfixed with horror, the apparition begins to fade.

"Wait!" Asha cries, reaching out instinctively. Her hand passes through empty air as the spirit vanishes completely.

The room temperature drops suddenly, and Asha shivers, wrapping her arms around herself. She's seen glimpses of strange shadows before, felt the weight of unseen eyes upon her. But this... this is different. The spirit is growing bolder, its manifestations more tangible.

A soft knock at the door makes Asha jump. "Nani?" Priya's voice calls out. "Is everything okay? I heard you shout."

Asha takes a deep breath, trying to compose herself before answering. "I'm fine, beta. Just... just a bad dream."

She hears Priya hesitate on the other side of the door. "Are you sure? Do you want me to come in?"

"No, no," Asha says quickly. "Go back to bed. We both need our rest."

As Priya's footsteps retreat down the hall, Asha sinks onto the edge of her bed. She glances warily at the mirror, half-expecting to see the spirit materialize again. But only her own tired face stares back at her.

Asha's gaze falls on the shelf where the cursed necklace sits, carefully wrapped in a silk cloth. Even hidden from view, she can feel its malevolent energy pulsing through the room.

"What have I done?" Asha whispers, a tear slipping down her cheek. "What have I brought upon us all?"

* * *

The next morning dawns gray and overcast, matching the somber mood that has settled over Asha's household. As she moves through her usual routine, Asha can't shake the feeling of being watched. Shadows seem to flicker at the corners of her vision, retreating whenever she turns to look directly at them.

Priya shuffles into the kitchen, dark circles prominent under her eyes. "Any word from Pandit Ravi Shankar?" she asks, her voice rough from lack of sleep.

Asha shakes her head. "Not yet, beta. But he said he'd come by this afternoon to continue our preparations for the ritual."

As if summoned by their conversation, a knock sounds at the door. Asha opens it to find not just Pandit Ravi Shankar, but a small group of villagers behind him. Their faces are drawn with worry and fear.

"Namaste, Asha-ji," one of the men says, wringing his hands nervously. "We... we need your help."

Asha ushers them inside, exchanging a concerned glance with Priya. As they gather in the living room, the villagers begin to share their stories. Crops withering overnight in fields that have always been fertile. Livestock falling ill with mysterious ailments that no veterinarian can explain. A general sense of unease that has settled over the entire village like a heavy fog.

"And now," a woman adds, her voice quavering, "people are starting to disappear."

Priya leans forward, her exhaustion momentarily forgotten. "Disappear? What do you mean?"

The woman wrings her hands. "My nephew, Arun. He went out to check on the goats two nights ago and never came back. We've searched everywhere, but it's like he just... vanished into thin air."

Murmurs of agreement ripple through the group. More stories emerge – a young couple who went for an evening walk and didn't return, an elderly man who stepped out to his garden and seemed to evaporate in broad daylight.

Asha's heart sinks as she listens to their tales. The curse's influence is spreading far beyond her home, affecting the entire community. She catches Pandit Ravi Shankar's eye, seeing her own guilt and worry reflected in his expression.

"We'll find a way to fix this," Asha assures the villagers, trying to project a confidence she doesn't entirely feel. "Pandit-ji is preparing a powerful ritual that will break the curse."

Hope flickers across their faces, but it's tinged with skepticism. Priya can't blame them – if someone had told her about curses and vengeful spirits a few weeks ago, she would have laughed it off as superstition.

As the villagers file out, their worried whispers trailing behind them, Priya turns to Pandit Ravi Shankar. "Is this ritual really going to work?" she asks bluntly. "Can it undo all of this damage?"

The priest's face is grave as he considers her question. "The ritual is our best hope," he says carefully. "But I won't lie to you – it won't be easy, and there are no guarantees. The curse has grown powerful, more so than I initially realized."

Priya nods, a determined set to her jaw. "Then we'd better make sure we do everything right. What's our next step?"

Before Pandit Ravi Shankar can answer, a loud bang echoes through the house. Priya jumps, her nerves already frayed from weeks of supernatural torment.

"What was that?" she asks, her voice pitched higher than usual.

Asha moves cautiously towards the hallway, peering around the corner. Another bang sounds, and she flinches back.

"It's the doors," she says, her voice shaking slightly. "They're... they're slamming shut on their own."

As if to emphasize her words, a series of thuds reverberate through the house – every door slamming closed in rapid succession. Picture frames rattle on the walls, and a vase topples from a side table, shattering on the floor.

Priya presses herself against the wall, her heart racing. "Is this part of the curse?" she asks, fighting to keep her voice steady.

Pandit Ravi Shankar nods grimly. "The spirit is growing stronger, more able to manipulate the physical world. We must act quickly."

He begins to lay out the components they've gathered, explaining the intricate steps of the ritual they'll need to perform. But even as he speaks, the atmosphere in the room grows heavier, more oppressive.

A sudden gust of wind sweeps through the living room, though all the windows are closed. It catches a framed family photo on the mantelpiece – a picture of Asha, Priya, and Priya's parents from happier times. The frame teeters for a moment, then crashes to the floor, glass splintering across the hardwood.

Priya moves to clean up the mess, but Asha grabs her arm. "Wait," she says, her voice barely above a whisper. "Listen."

They fall silent, straining their ears. In the quiet, they become aware of a sound that's been a constant backdrop to life in the village – the incessant barking of the neighbor's dog. But now...

"It's stopped," Priya says, a chill running down her spine. The silence is deafening, unnatural.

Pandit Ravi Shankar's face is grim as he surveys the room. "The presence is growing stronger," he says. "We're running out of time."

As if in response to his words, the temperature in the room plummets. Priya's breath fogs in the air, and goosebumps erupt along her arms. A low, ominous rumble builds from somewhere deep within the house.

"What's happening?" Asha asks, her voice trembling as she clutches Priya's arm.

Before anyone can respond, the rumble crescendos into a deafening roar. The floor beneath their feet begins to tremble, and objects around the room start to rattle and shake.

"Get down!" Pandit Ravi Shankar shouts, pulling Asha and Priya to the ground as a vase hurtles through the air where their heads had been moments before.

Chaos erupts around them. Furniture slides across the floor as if pushed by invisible hands. Books fly off shelves, their pages fluttering wildly. The temperature continues to drop, frost crystallizing on the windows despite the warm day outside.

In the midst of the mayhem, a chilling howl fills the air – not the bark of a dog, but something decidedly more sinister. It's a sound that raises the hair on the back of Priya's neck, primal and full of malice.

"The spirit!" Pandit Ravi Shankar yells over the cacophony. "It's manifesting!"

As if summoned by his words, a dark, swirling mass begins to coalesce in the center of the room. It writhes and pulses, gradually taking on a vaguely humanoid shape. Two pinpricks of sickly green light appear where eyes should be, fixing on the huddled group with unmistakable hatred.

Priya feels a scream building in her throat, but it emerges as little more than a whimper. This is the entity from her nightmares, more terrifying in reality than she could have ever imagined.

The spirit lets out another bone-chilling howl and lunges towards them. Pandit Ravi Shankar reacts instantly, throwing himself in front of Asha and Priya. He begins to chant rapidly in Sanskrit, his hands moving in intricate gestures.

A shimmering barrier of golden light springs up between them and the entity. The spirit slams against it, causing the barrier to flicker and waver, but it holds – for now.

"The protective amulets!" Pandit Ravi Shankar shouts, strain evident in his voice as he maintains the barrier. "In my bag – quickly!"

Priya scrambles for the priest's satchel, her hands shaking as she rummages through it. She pulls out three small pouches, each containing a blessed amulet.

"Put them on!" Pandit Ravi Shankar instructs, sweat beading on his brow as the spirit continues its assault on the barrier.

Priya helps Asha secure her amulet before donning her own. The moment the cool metal touches her skin, she feels a surge of energy coursing through her. The oppressive weight of the spirit's presence lessens slightly, allowing her to think more clearly.

"Now what?" Priya asks, her voice steadier than she feels.

"We need to banish it – force it back to wherever it came from," Pandit Ravi Shankar says. "Join hands and repeat after me!"

As they form a circle, hands clasped tightly, the priest begins to recite an ancient mantra. Priya and Asha stumble over the unfamiliar words at first, but soon find the rhythm. Their voices blend together, growing stronger with each repetition.

The spirit shrieks in fury, redoubling its efforts to break through the barrier. Objects whirl around the room in a deadly cyclone, smashing against walls and shattering into pieces. The very foundations of the house seem to groan under the onslaught.

But as they continue to chant, Priya notices a change. The spirit's form begins to waver, its edges becoming less defined. Its howls take on a note of desperation rather than rage.

"Keep going!" Pandit Ravi Shankar encourages them, his own voice hoarse from the prolonged chanting.

With one final, ear-splitting shriek, the spirit's form implodes. The swirling mass of darkness collapses in on itself, vanishing with a thunderclap that shakes the entire house.

In the sudden silence that follows, the only sound is their heavy breathing. Priya's legs give out, and she sinks to the floor, trembling from exhaustion and residual fear.

"Is it... is it gone?" Asha asks hesitantly, looking around at the devastation of her once-tidy living room.

Pandit Ravi Shankar nods slowly, his face drawn with fatigue. "For now," he says. "But this was only a manifestation. The curse itself remains, and it will only grow stronger."

As the adrenaline fades, Priya feels the full weight of what they've just experienced crashing down on her. Tears well up in her eyes, a mix of relief and overwhelming fear for what's still to come.

"How can we possibly fight this?" she whispers, her voice breaking. "It's too powerful."

Asha kneels beside her granddaughter, wrapping an arm around her shoulders. "Together," she says firmly. "We'll face it together, beta. And we will find a way to break this curse."

Pandit Ravi Shankar nods in agreement, but there's a flicker of something in his eyes – guilt? uncertainty? – that makes Priya uneasy.

"There's something you're not telling us, isn't there?" she asks, fixing the priest with a steady gaze.

The priest hesitates, conflict evident on his face. Finally, he sighs heavily, his shoulders slumping. "There is... there is something I must confess," he says quietly.

Asha and Priya exchange worried glances as Pandit Ravi Shankar settles himself on a nearby chair, his expression grave.

"The truth is," he begins, his voice heavy with regret, "I have known about this curse for years. It's not just a village myth, as I once believed. It's very real, and very dangerous."

The revelation hangs in the air between them, shattering the trust they had placed in the priest. Priya feels a surge of anger rising within her, temporarily overriding her fear and exhaustion.

"You knew?" she demands, her voice rising. "All this time, you knew what we were dealing with, and you said nothing?"

Asha places a calming hand on Priya's arm, but her own expression is one of hurt and betrayal. "Why, Pandit-ji?" she asks softly. "Why keep this from us?"

Pandit Ravi Shankar bows his head, unable to meet their eyes. "I thought... I thought I was protecting the village," he says. "The curse had been dormant for so long, I convinced myself it was nothing more than an old wives' tale. I feared that speaking of it would only cause panic."

He looks up, his eyes filled with remorse. "I was wrong. I should have prepared you, warned you of the danger. And for that, I am truly sorry."

The room falls silent as Asha and Priya process this new information. The betrayal stings, compounding the fear and uncertainty that have plagued them since the necklace was first unearthed.

"What else haven't you told us?" Priya asks, her voice cold. "What else do we need to know about this curse?"

Pandit Ravi Shankar straightens, seeming to come to a decision. "Everything," he says firmly. "It's time you knew everything. The origin of the curse, its true nature, and why it's so difficult to break. Only then can we hope to face what's coming."

As the priest begins to speak, weaving a tale of ancient betrayals and dark magic, Priya and Asha listen intently. The sun sinks lower in the sky outside, casting long shadows across the room – a stark reminder of the darkness that threatens to engulf them all.

4 Echoes of the Ancients

Priya stares out the window, her fingers tracing idle patterns on the glass. Outside, dark clouds loom on the horizon, mirroring the oppressive atmosphere that has settled over the village. She feels a chill run down her spine, goosebumps erupting along her arms despite the warmth of the day.

"Nani," she calls out, her voice barely above a whisper. "Something's wrong."

Asha hurries into the room, concern etched on her weathered face. "What is it, beta?"

Priya gestures towards the window. "Look at the sky. It's not natural."

Asha peers outside, her brow furrowing. The clouds roil and churn, tinged with an eerie greenish hue. As they watch, a bolt of lightning splits the sky, followed by a thunderclap that shakes the very foundations of the house.

"We need to speak with Pandit Ravi," Asha says, her voice tight with worry. "This is no ordinary storm."

They make their way to the village temple, the wind whipping at their clothes and tearing at their hair. The usually bustling streets are eerily empty, villagers having retreated indoors to escape the ominous weather.

Pandit Ravi meets them at the temple entrance, his face grave. "I've been expecting you," he says, ushering them inside. "The curse is growing stronger by the hour."

Priya feels a surge of frustration. "What can we do? We've tried everything!"

The priest's eyes flicker with an emotion Priya can't quite place – guilt? Fear? "Not everything," he says quietly. "There is... there is one more ritual we can attempt. But it's dangerous."

Asha grips Priya's hand tightly. "Tell us," she demands. "Whatever it is, we'll face it together."

Pandit Ravi nods solemnly. "It's an ancient rite, passed down through generations of priests. It requires great sacrifice and carries great risk. But if successful, it could banish the spirit and break the curse once and for all."

As he begins to explain the intricacies of the ritual, another thunderclap rocks the temple. The flames of the sacred lamps flicker wildly, casting grotesque shadows on the walls.

Priya shivers, pulling her shawl tighter around her shoulders. "What do we need to do?"

"First," Pandit Ravi says, his voice barely audible over the howling wind outside, "we must gather the necessary components. Rare herbs, sacred relics, items of power. They are scattered throughout the village and surrounding areas."

Asha straightens, determination flashing in her eyes. "Tell us where to find them. We'll leave at once."

The priest shakes his head. "Not you, Asha-ji. The journey will be perilous. Priya and I will go. You must stay here, where it's safer."

Priya opens her mouth to protest, but Asha silences her with a look. "He's right, beta. I'll only slow you down. But promise me you'll be careful."

Swallowing hard, Priya nods. "I promise, Nani. We'll be back before you know it."

As Pandit Ravi gathers supplies for their quest, Priya pulls her grandmother into a tight embrace. "I love you," she whispers fiercely.

Asha cups Priya's face in her weathered hands. "And I love you, my brave girl. Remember, no matter what happens, you carry the strength of our ancestors within you. Trust in that strength."

With one last lingering look, Priya follows Pandit Ravi out into the raging storm. The wind howls around them, driving icy raindrops against their skin like tiny needles.

"Where to first?" Priya shouts over the tempest.

Pandit Ravi points towards the dense forest at the village's edge. "The sacred grove," he calls back. "We need leaves from the ancient bodhi tree."

They stumble through the muddy streets, struggling to keep their footing on the slippery ground. As they near the forest's edge, a bone-chilling howl rises above the storm's cacophony.

Priya freezes, her heart pounding. "What was that?"

The priest's face is grim. "The spirit grows bolder. We must hurry."

They plunge into the forest, branches whipping at their faces and tearing at their clothes. The darkness is almost absolute, broken only by intermittent flashes of lightning that illuminate their path in stark, terrifying clarity.

As they near the sacred grove, the air grows thick and heavy, pressing down on them like a physical weight. Priya's breaths come in short, sharp gasps, her lungs straining against the oppressive atmosphere.

"There," Pandit Ravi wheezes, pointing to a massive tree looming before them. Its gnarled branches reach towards the sky like grasping fingers, leaves rustling ominously despite the lack of wind in the grove.

Priya approaches the tree cautiously, her hand outstretched. As her fingers brush against the rough bark, a jolt of energy surges through her body. She gasps, stumbling backward.

"What-" she begins, but her words are cut short by a blood-curdling scream that echoes through the grove.

Pandit Ravi's eyes widen in terror. "The spirit! It's here!"

A dark, writhing mass materializes before them, pulsing with malevolent energy. Two pinpricks of sickly green light fix upon them, filled with an otherworldly hatred.

"Run!" Pandit Ravi shouts, shoving Priya towards the tree. "Get the leaves! I'll hold it off!"

Priya scrambles up the tree, her heart pounding in her ears. Behind her, she hears the priest chanting rapidly, his voice strained with effort. The spirit shrieks in fury, the sound sending shivers down Priya's spine.

Her fingers close around a cluster of leaves, and she tears them free. "I've got them!" she yells, beginning her descent.

But as she reaches the lowest branch, she sees Pandit Ravi on his knees, his face ashen. The spirit looms over him, its form growing larger and more defined with each passing second.

Without thinking, Priya leaps from the tree, landing between the priest and the entity. She holds the bodhi leaves before her like a shield, her voice shaking as she recites the protective mantra Asha taught her as a child.

To her amazement, the spirit recoils, shrieking in pain. It retreats, its form dissipating into the shadows of the grove.

Priya helps Pandit Ravi to his feet, her legs trembling with residual fear and adrenaline. "Are you alright?" she asks, searching his face for signs of injury.

The priest nods weakly. "Thanks to you," he says, his voice hoarse. "You saved my life."

They make their way back through the forest, the storm seeming to intensify with each step. By the time they reach the village, they're soaked to the bone and shivering uncontrollably.

Asha rushes to meet them at the temple door, her face etched with worry. "What happened?" she demands, ushering them inside. "You were gone for hours!"

As Priya recounts their harrowing experience in the grove, Asha's expression grows increasingly grave. "The spirit is growing stronger," she murmurs. "We're running out of time."

Pandit Ravi nods solemnly. "We have the bodhi leaves, but there are still more components to gather. And with each passing hour, the danger grows."

A heavy silence falls over the temple, broken only by the howling wind outside. Priya feels a weight settling on her shoulders, the enormity of their task threatening to overwhelm her.

But as she looks at her grandmother's determined face and the resolve in Pandit Ravi's eyes, she feels a flicker of hope. They've come this far together. Whatever challenges lie ahead, they'll face them as one.

"What's next?" Priya asks, squaring her shoulders. "Where do we go from here?"

Pandit Ravi unfurls an ancient map on the temple floor, its edges crumbling with age. "The sacred spring in the hills," he says, pointing to a spot marked with faded ink. "Its waters have powerful purifying properties. We'll need them for the final ritual."

Asha frowns, studying the map. "That's a treacherous journey, especially in this weather. Are you sure there's no other way?"

The priest shakes his head grimly. "I'm afraid not. The spring's waters are essential. Without them, we have no hope of breaking the curse."

Priya takes a deep breath, steeling herself. "Then we have no choice. When do we leave?"

"First light tomorrow," Pandit Ravi says. "We'll need all the daylight we can get to navigate the mountain paths."

As they prepare for the perilous journey ahead, gathering supplies and studying the ancient map, Priya can't shake the feeling that they're being watched. Shadows seem to flicker at the corners of her vision, retreating whenever she turns to look directly at them.

"Nani," she whispers, pulling Asha aside. "Do you feel it? Like there are eyes on us, all the time?"

Asha nods, her face grim. "The spirit grows bolder. It knows we seek to destroy it."

A chill runs down Priya's spine. "What if... what if we can't do this? What if we're not strong enough?"

Asha cups Priya's face in her weathered hands, her eyes blazing with fierce determination. "Listen to me, beta. You come from a long line of strong women. Our ancestors faced challenges just as great as this, and they prevailed. That same strength flows in your veins. Never doubt it."

Priya nods, drawing strength from her grandmother's unwavering faith. As they return to their preparations, she notices Pandit Ravi watching them with an unreadable expression.

"Is everything alright?" she asks, approaching the priest.

He starts, as if pulled from deep thought. "Yes, yes," he says quickly. "Just... thinking about the journey ahead."

But there's something in his eyes – a flicker of guilt, perhaps? – that makes Priya uneasy. Before she can press further, however, a commotion outside draws their attention.

They rush to the temple entrance to find a group of villagers gathered, their faces drawn with fear and desperation.

"Pandit-ji," one man calls out, wringing his hands. "You must help us! Strange things are happening all over the village. Crops withering overnight, livestock falling ill..."

Another woman steps forward, her voice quavering. "And people... people are starting to disappear."

A murmur of fear ripples through the crowd. Priya exchanges a worried glance with Asha. The curse's influence is spreading far beyond their home, affecting the entire community.

Pandit Ravi raises his hands, calling for calm. "Please, good people. I understand your fear. But I assure you, we are working to resolve this. We leave at dawn to gather the final components needed to break the curse."

The villagers hang on his every word, hope warring with skepticism on their faces. Priya can't blame them – if someone had told her about curses and vengeful spirits a few weeks ago, she would have laughed it off as superstition.

As the crowd disperses, their worried whispers trailing behind them, Priya turns to Pandit Ravi. "Is this ritual really going to work?" she asks bluntly. "Can it undo all of this damage?"

The priest's face is grave as he considers her question. "The ritual is our best hope," he says carefully. "But I won't lie to you – it won't be easy, and there are no guarantees. The curse has grown powerful, more so than I initially realized."

Priya nods, a determined set to her jaw. "Then we'd better make sure we do everything right. What's our next step?"

Before Pandit Ravi can answer, a loud bang echoes through the temple. Priya jumps, her nerves already frayed from weeks of supernatural torment.

"What was that?" she asks, her voice pitched higher than usual.

Asha moves cautiously towards the inner sanctum, peering around the corner. Another bang sounds, and she flinches back.

"It's the doors," she says, her voice shaking slightly. "They're... they're slamming shut on their own."

As if to emphasize her words, a series of thuds reverberate through the temple – every door slamming closed in rapid succession. The sacred lamps flicker wildly, and a cold wind whips through the space, though all windows are tightly shut.

Priya presses herself against the wall, her heart racing. "Is this part of the curse?" she asks, fighting to keep her voice steady.

Pandit Ravi nods grimly. "The spirit is growing stronger, more able to manipulate the physical world. We must act quickly."

He begins to lay out the components they've gathered, explaining the intricate steps of the ritual they'll need to perform. But even as he speaks, the atmosphere in the temple grows heavier, more oppressive.

A sudden gust of wind sweeps through the space, extinguishing several of the sacred lamps. It catches a framed image of a deity on the wall – an ancient painting that has hung in the temple for generations. The frame teeters for a moment, then crashes to the floor, glass splintering across the stone.

Priya moves to clean up the mess, but Asha grabs her arm. "Wait," she says, her voice barely above a whisper. "Listen."

They fall silent, straining their ears. In the quiet, they become aware of a sound that's been a constant backdrop to life in the village – the incessant barking of the stray dogs that roam the streets. But now...

"It's stopped," Priya says, a chill running down her spine. The silence is deafening, unnatural.

Pandit Ravi's face is grim as he surveys the temple. "The presence is growing stronger," he says. "We're running out of time."

As if in response to his words, the temperature in the room plummets. Priya's breath fogs in the air, and goosebumps erupt along her arms. A low, ominous rumble builds from somewhere deep within the temple's foundations.

"What's happening?" Asha asks, her voice trembling as she clutches Priya's arm.

Before anyone can respond, the rumble crescendos into a deafening roar. The floor beneath their feet begins to tremble, and objects around the temple start to rattle and shake.

"Get down!" Pandit Ravi shouts, pulling Asha and Priya to the ground as a heavy brass bell hurtles through the air where their heads had been moments before.

Chaos erupts around them. Statues slide across the floor as if pushed by invisible hands. Sacred texts fly off shelves, their pages fluttering wildly. The temperature continues to drop, frost crystallizing on the windows despite the warm day outside.

In the midst of the mayhem, a chilling howl fills the air – not the bark of a dog, but something decidedly more sinister. It's a sound that raises the hair on the back of Priya's neck, primal and full of malice.

"The spirit!" Pandit Ravi yells over the cacophony. "It's manifesting!"

As if summoned by his words, a dark, swirling mass begins to coalesce in the center of the temple. It writhes and pulses, gradually taking on a vaguely humanoid shape. Two pinpricks of sickly green light appear where eyes should be, fixing on the huddled group with unmistakable hatred.

Priya feels a scream building in her throat, but it emerges as little more than a whimper. This is the entity from her nightmares, more terrifying in reality than she could have ever imagined.

The spirit lets out another bone-chilling howl and lunges towards them. Pandit Ravi reacts instantly, throwing himself in front of Asha and Priya. He begins to chant rapidly in Sanskrit, his hands moving in intricate gestures.

A shimmering barrier of golden light springs up between them and the entity. The spirit slams against it, causing the barrier to flicker and waver, but it holds – for now.

"The protective amulets!" Pandit Ravi shouts, strain evident in his voice as he maintains the barrier. "In my bag – quickly!"

Priya scrambles for the priest's satchel, her hands shaking as she rummages through it. She pulls out three small pouches, each containing a blessed amulet.

"Put them on!" Pandit Ravi instructs, sweat beading on his brow as the spirit continues its assault on the barrier.

Priya helps Asha secure her amulet before donning her own. The moment the cool metal touches her skin, she feels a surge of energy coursing through her. The oppressive weight of the spirit's presence lessens slightly, allowing her to think more clearly.

"Now what?" Priya asks, her voice steadier than she feels.

"We need to banish it – force it back to wherever it came from," Pandit Ravi says. "Join hands and repeat after me!"

As they form a circle, hands clasped tightly, the priest begins to recite an ancient mantra. Priya and Asha stumble over the unfamiliar words at first, but soon find the rhythm. Their voices blend together, growing stronger with each repetition.

The spirit shrieks in fury, redoubling its efforts to break through the barrier. Objects whirl around the temple in a deadly cyclone, smashing against walls and shattering into pieces. The very foundations of the building seem to groan under the onslaught.

But as they continue to chant, Priya notices a change. The spirit's form begins to waver, its edges becoming less defined. Its howls take on a note of desperation rather than rage.

"Keep going!" Pandit Ravi encourages them, his own voice hoarse from the prolonged chanting.

With one final, ear-splitting shriek, the spirit's form implodes. The swirling mass of darkness collapses in on itself, vanishing with a thunderclap that shakes the entire temple.

In the sudden silence that follows, the only sound is their heavy breathing. Priya's legs give out, and she sinks to the floor, trembling from exhaustion and residual fear.

"Is it... is it gone?" Asha asks hesitantly, looking around at the devastation of the once-pristine temple.

Pandit Ravi nods slowly, his face drawn with fatigue. "For now," he says. "But this was only a manifestation. The curse itself remains, and it will only grow stronger."

As the adrenaline fades, Priya feels the full weight of what they've just experienced crashing down on her. Tears well up in her eyes, a mix of relief and overwhelming fear for what's still to come.

"How can we possibly fight this?" she whispers, her voice breaking. "It's too powerful."

Asha kneels beside her granddaughter, wrapping an arm around her shoulders. "Together," she says firmly. "We'll face it together, beta. And we will find a way to break this curse."

Pandit Ravi nods in agreement, but there's a flicker of something in his eyes – guilt? uncertainty? – that makes Priya uneasy.

"There's something you're not telling us, isn't there?" she asks, fixing the priest with a steady gaze.

The priest hesitates, conflict evident on his face. Finally, he sighs heavily, his shoulders slumping. "There is... there is something I must confess," he says quietly.

Asha and Priya exchange worried glances as Pandit Ravi settles himself on a nearby chair, his expression grave.

"The truth is," he begins, his voice heavy with regret, "I have known about this curse for years. It's not just a village myth, as I once believed. It's very real, and very dangerous."

The revelation hangs in the air between them, shattering the trust they had placed in the priest. Priya feels a surge of anger rising within her, temporarily overriding her fear and exhaustion.

"You knew?" she demands, her voice rising. "All this time, you knew what we were dealing with, and you said nothing?"

Asha places a calming hand on Priya's arm, but her own expression is one of hurt and betrayal. "Why, Pandit-ji?" she asks softly. "Why keep this from us?"

Pandit Ravi bows his head, unable to meet their eyes. "I thought... I thought I was protecting the village," he says. "The curse had been dormant for so long, I convinced myself it was nothing more than an old wives' tale. I feared that speaking of it would only cause panic."

He looks up, his eyes filled with remorse. "I was wrong. I should have prepared you, warned you of the danger. And for that, I am truly sorry."

The room falls silent as Asha and Priya process this new information. The betrayal stings, compounding the fear and uncertainty that have plagued them since the necklace was first unearthed.

"What else haven't you told us?" Priya asks, her voice cold. "What else do we need to know about this curse?"

Pandit Ravi straightens, seeming to come to a decision. "Everything," he says firmly. "It's time you knew everything. The origin of the curse, its true nature, and why it's so difficult to break. Only then can we hope to face what's coming."

As the priest begins to speak, weaving a tale of ancient betrayals and dark magic, Priya and Asha listen intently. The sun sinks lower in the sky outside, casting long shadows across the temple – a stark reminder of the darkness that threatens to engulf them all.

"It began centuries ago," Pandit Ravi says, his voice taking on a rhythmic cadence of a practiced storyteller. "In this very village, there lived a woman named Amara. She was known for her beauty, her wisdom, and her mastery of the mystical arts."

Priya leans forward, drawn into the tale despite her lingering anger. "Was she a witch?"

The priest shakes his head. "Not in the way you might think. Amara was a healer, a protector of the village. She used her gifts to ward off evil spirits, cure illnesses, and ensure bountiful harvests."

"But something went wrong," Asha says softly, intuiting the direction of the story.

Pandit Ravi nods grimly. "Indeed. Amara fell in love with a man from a neighboring village. Their love was pure and true, but it aroused jealousy in the heart of our village's leader. He coveted Amara for himself."

The priest's eyes grow distant, as if seeing the events unfold before him. "The leader conspired with others who feared Amara's power. They accused her of dark sorcery, turning the villagers against her. On a moonless night, they dragged her from her home and..."

He trails off, swallowing hard. Priya feels a chill run down her spine, already guessing the horrific conclusion.

"They killed her," Asha whispers, her face pale.

Pandit Ravi nods. "But as she died, Amara uttered a curse. She vowed that her spirit would never rest, that she would return to exact vengeance on the descendants of those who had wronged her."

Priya's mind races, connecting the dots. "The necklace," she says. "It was hers, wasn't it?"

"Yes," the priest confirms. "It was her most prized possession, imbued with her power. When it was buried with her, it became a vessel for her vengeful spirit."

A heavy silence falls over the temple as the full weight of the situation sinks in. Priya feels a mix of emotions churning within her – anger at the injustice done to Amara, fear of the power they're up against, and a growing sense of determination to set things right.

"So how do we break the curse?" she asks, her voice steady despite the trembling in her hands.

Pandit Ravi's expression grows grave. "That's where things become... complicated. The ritual I spoke of earlier – it's not just about banishing the spirit. To truly break the curse, we must offer Amara's spirit the justice she was denied in life."

Asha leans forward, her brow furrowed. "What do you mean?"

The priest takes a deep breath. "We must uncover the truth of what happened all those centuries ago. Find evidence of Amara's innocence, expose the lies that led to her death. And then... then we must make amends on behalf of the entire village."

Priya feels a spark of hope ignite within her. "That doesn't sound so impossible," she says. "Surely there must be records, stories passed down through generations..."

But Pandit Ravi shakes his head. "Those who conspired against Amara were thorough. They destroyed every trace of her existence, rewrote the village's history. Finding the truth will be no easy task."

"And the spirit won't make it easy for us," Asha adds softly. "It will fight us every step of the way."

The priest nods grimly. "Which is why we must act quickly. With each passing day, Amara's spirit grows stronger, more consumed by hatred. If we don't break the curse soon, I fear there will be nothing left of the woman she once was – only a force of vengeance that will destroy everything in its path."

As if to punctuate his words, a cold wind sweeps through the temple, extinguishing the few remaining lamps. In the sudden darkness, Priya swears she sees a figure standing in the corner – a woman with long, flowing hair and eyes that glow with an otherworldly light. She blinks, and the apparition vanishes.

"So what do we do now?" Priya asks, her voice barely above a whisper.

Pandit Ravi's face is set with determination. "We prepare for the journey ahead. We'll need to delve into the village's past, seek out hidden truths, and face whatever challenges Amara's spirit throws our way."

He turns to Priya, his eyes intense. "Are you ready for this? Once we begin, there's no turning back."

Priya takes a deep breath, squaring her shoulders. She thinks of the terror of the past weeks, of the village suffering under the curse's influence. But she also thinks of Amara – a woman wronged, crying out for justice across the centuries.

"I'm ready," she says firmly. "Whatever it takes, we're going to break this curse and set things right."

Asha reaches out, taking Priya's hand in her own. "We'll face this together, beta. Just as we always have."

As they begin to discuss their plans, mapping out the challenges ahead, Priya can't shake the feeling that they're being watched. In the shadows of the temple, unseen by the three humans, a spectral figure lingers. Its eyes, filled with a mix of sorrow and rage, follow their every move. The battle for the village's past – and its future – has only just begun.

5 Echoes of Desperation

Priya stands at the window, her fingers pressed against the cool glass. Outside, the village is shrouded in an unnatural twilight, though it's barely past noon. Shadows creep along the edges of buildings, writhing and twisting in ways that defy explanation. A chill runs down her spine as she spots a ghostly figure flitting between houses, there and gone in the blink of an eye.

"It's getting worse," she murmurs, her breath fogging the window.

Behind her, Pandit Ravi Shankar nods grimly. "The full moon approaches. The veil between worlds grows thin."

Priya turns, frustration etched on her face. "But what does that mean? How do we stop it?"

The priest opens his mouth to respond, but a commotion outside draws their attention. Villagers are gathering in the street, their voices raised in a cacophony of fear and anger. Priya pushes open the window, straining to hear.

"...can't go on like this!" one man shouts. "My crops are withering in the fields!"

"My goats won't eat," a woman adds, her voice trembling. "It's like they can sense something evil..."

"Where's Pandit-ji?" another demands. "He's supposed to protect us!"

Priya's stomach twists. The fear is palpable, a living thing that threatens to consume the entire village. She glances at Pandit Ravi Shankar, seeing the weight of responsibility heavy on his shoulders.

"We need to do something," she says. "They're terrified."

The priest nods, straightening his robes. "I'll speak with them. Try to calm their fears."

As he moves towards the door, a piercing scream cuts through the air. Priya's heart leaps into her throat. "Nani!" she gasps, already racing towards her grandmother's room.

She bursts through the door to find Asha thrashing in her bed, eyes wide with terror. "No, no, no," the old woman moans, her hands clawing at unseen assailants. "Stay away!"

"Nani, it's me!" Priya grabs her grandmother's hands, shocked at how cold they feel. "You're safe, I'm here."

But Asha doesn't seem to hear her. Her skin is ashen, beaded with sweat. As Priya watches in horror, dark veins begin to spread across her grandmother's face, pulsing with an otherworldly energy.

"Pandit-ji!" Priya screams, panic rising in her chest. "Something's wrong with Nani!"

The priest rushes in, his face paling as he takes in the scene. He places a hand on Asha's forehead, muttering a quick prayer. "The curse," he says grimly. "It's affecting her directly now."

Priya feels as if the floor has dropped out from beneath her. "What do we do?" she asks, her voice small and frightened.

Pandit Ravi Shankar shakes his head. "I... I don't know. This is beyond anything I've encountered before."

As if to punctuate his words, Asha lets out another gut-wrenching scream. The sound seems to reverberate through the house, setting every nerve in Priya's body on edge. She stumbles back, her hands shaking uncontrollably.

"This can't be happening," she whispers, squeezing her eyes shut. "This can't be real."

But when she opens them again, the nightmare hasn't faded. Asha continues to writhe on the bed, locked in some internal battle they can't see or understand. The dark veins have spread further, a web of corruption creeping across her skin.

Priya's vision blurs, the room spinning around her. She grabs onto the doorframe for support, her breath coming in short, sharp gasps. The walls seem to close in, shadows dancing at the edges of her vision.

"Priya?" Pandit Ravi Shankar's voice sounds distant, muffled. "Are you alright?"

She tries to respond, but the words won't come. Instead, a high-pitched ringing fills her ears. The shadows in the room coalesce, taking on monstrous shapes. Priya blinks rapidly, trying to clear her vision, but the apparitions only grow more vivid.

A skeletal figure looms over Asha's bed, its bony fingers reaching for her grandmother. Priya wants to scream, to run, to do something, but her body won't respond. She's frozen, trapped in a waking nightmare.

"No," she manages to choke out. "Leave her alone!"

The skeletal figure turns its hollow eyes towards her. Its jaw unhinges, stretching impossibly wide as it lets out a silent scream. Priya's knees buckle, and she collapses to the floor.

"Priya!" Pandit Ravi Shankar's voice cuts through the fog of terror. She feels his hands on her shoulders, shaking her gently. "Come back to us, child. It's not real."

Gradually, the monstrous visions fade. Priya blinks, finding herself curled up on the floor, trembling violently. The priest kneels beside her, concern etched on his face.

"What... what happened?" she asks, her voice hoarse.

"The spirit is growing stronger," Pandit Ravi Shankar says grimly. "It's affecting your mind, making you see things that aren't there."

Priya struggles to sit up, her limbs feeling like lead. "But Nani... is she...?"

They both turn to look at Asha. The old woman has fallen still, her chest rising and falling with shallow breaths. The dark veins have receded slightly, but her skin remains pale and clammy.

"She's stable for now," the priest says. "But we're running out of time. The curse is taking its toll on both of you."

A commotion from outside draws their attention. The villagers' voices have risen again, more insistent this time. Priya can make out her name being called, along with demands to see Pandit Ravi Shankar.

"They're getting restless," she says, pushing herself to her feet despite the lingering dizziness. "We need to talk to them."

The priest nods, his expression grave. "Yes, but we must be careful. Fear can turn people against each other. We cannot let that happen."

Together, they make their way to the front door. Priya takes a deep breath, steeling herself for what's to come. As Pandit Ravi Shankar opens the door, they're met with a sea of frightened, angry faces.

"There they are!" someone shouts. "Tell us what's going on!"

"Why aren't you doing something to stop this?" another demands.

The accusations fly thick and fast. Priya feels overwhelmed by the onslaught of fear and desperation. She glances at Pandit Ravi Shankar, silently urging him to say something, anything, to calm the crowd.

The priest raises his hands, his voice carrying over the clamor. "Please, my friends. I understand your fear. But we must remain united in the face of this challenge."

"Challenge?" a man scoffs. "This is more than a challenge, Pandit-ji. This is a curse!"

Murmurs of agreement ripple through the crowd. Priya steps forward, her heart pounding. "It is a curse," she says, her voice shaking slightly. "But we're doing everything we can to break it."

"And what exactly are you doing?" a woman demands. "My children are terrified to sleep at night. We see... things in the shadows. How long must we endure this?"

Priya exchanges a glance with Pandit Ravi Shankar. They can't reveal everything – the knowledge of the necklace, the full extent of the danger – but they need to give the villagers something to hold onto.

"We've discovered a potential solution," the priest says carefully. "An ancient charm that may protect us from the curse's influence."

A spark of hope flickers across some faces, but others remain skeptical. "Where is this charm?" someone calls out. "Why haven't you used it yet?"

Priya takes a deep breath. "It's hidden in the sacred tree at the edge of the village. We're preparing to retrieve it, but it's dangerous. The... the spirit doesn't want us to succeed."

A hush falls over the crowd as her words sink in. Priya can see the fear warring with hope in their eyes. She silently prays that they'll choose hope.

After what feels like an eternity, an elderly man steps forward. "What can we do to help?" he asks, his voice wavering but determined.

Relief washes over Priya. She looks to Pandit Ravi Shankar, who nods encouragingly. "We need you to stay strong," she says. "Look out for each other. And most importantly, don't lose faith. We will break this curse, I promise you."

The tension in the air eases slightly. It's not a solution, not yet, but it's something for the villagers to cling to. As the crowd begins to disperse, Priya feels a flicker of hope. Maybe, just maybe, they can get through this.

But as she turns to go back inside, a wave of dizziness washes over her. The world tilts alarmingly, and she stumbles. Pandit Ravi Shankar catches her arm, steadying her.

"Priya?" he asks, concern evident in his voice. "What's wrong?"

She shakes her head, trying to clear the fog that's descended over her mind. "I don't... I'm not sure. I feel strange."

The priest's frown deepens. "The curse is affecting you more strongly now. We must act quickly."

Priya nods, fighting back another wave of nausea. "The charm," she says. "We need to get it. Now."

Pandit Ravi Shankar hesitates, glancing back at the house where Asha lies ill. "It's dangerous," he warns. "In your condition..."

"We don't have a choice," Priya interrupts, her voice stronger than she feels. "Nani is getting worse. The village is falling apart. We have to do something."

After a moment's consideration, the priest nods. "Very well. But we must be cautious. The spirit will not give up its power easily."

As they gather the supplies they'll need for the journey to the sacred tree, Priya can't shake the feeling that they're walking into a trap. But with her grandmother's labored breathing echoing in her ears and the memory of the villagers' frightened faces fresh in her mind, she knows they have no other option.

The fate of the entire village rests on their shoulders. And as the sun begins to set, casting long shadows across the land, Priya steels herself for the challenges that lie ahead. Whatever the spirit throws at them, she's determined to face it head-on. For Nani, for the village, and for herself.

6 The Battle for the Charm

The path to the sacred tree stretches before them, a winding trail that seems to disappear into the gathering gloom. Priya adjusts the strap of her backpack, wincing as a dull ache pulses through her temples. Beside her, Pandit Ravi Shankar mutters a quiet prayer, his weathered hands clutching a small pouch of sacred ash.

"Are you ready?" he asks, his eyes searching Priya's face.

She nods, swallowing hard. "As ready as I'll ever be."

They set off, their footsteps crunching on the dry leaves that carpet the forest floor. The air grows thick and heavy as they move deeper into the woods, carrying with it the scent of decay and something darker, something unnatural.

Priya's skin prickles with goosebumps. Every shadow seems to writhe and twist, hinting at monstrous shapes just beyond the edge of vision. She shakes her head, trying to clear the fog that threatens to cloud her mind.

"Stay focused," Pandit Ravi Shankar says softly. "The spirit will try to confuse us, to lead us astray."

As if in response to his words, a low moan echoes through the trees. Priya freezes, her heart hammering against her ribs. "Did you hear that?"

The priest nods grimly. "It's starting. We must hurry."

They quicken their pace, branches whipping at their faces as they push through the undergrowth. The moaning grows louder, joined by a cacophony of whispers that seem to come from everywhere and nowhere at once.

Priya stumbles, her foot catching on an exposed root. As she rights herself, she gasps in horror. The trees around them have changed, their bark now resembling twisted, agonized faces. Eyes blink open in knotholes, mouths gape in silent screams.

"It's not real," she whispers, squeezing her eyes shut. "It's just the curse playing tricks."

But when she opens them again, the nightmarish visages remain. Pandit Ravi Shankar grabs her hand, pulling her forward. "Don't look," he urges. "Keep moving."

They press on, the forest growing denser with each step. The whispers coalesce into words, taunting and pleading in turn. Priya hears her grandmother's voice calling out in pain, then the frightened cries of the villagers.

"Please," she whimpers, tears stinging her eyes. "Make it stop."

Pandit Ravi Shankar's grip on her hand tightens. "It's not real," he reminds her. "Focus on why we're here. Think of Asha, of the village."

Priya nods, gritting her teeth. She forces herself to put one foot in front of the other, ignoring the phantoms that dance at the edges of her vision.

Suddenly, the priest comes to an abrupt halt. Priya nearly collides with him, her breath catching in her throat as she sees what lies ahead.

The sacred tree looms before them, its massive trunk twisted into impossible shapes. Unlike the other trees, this one seems all too real, pulsing with an otherworldly energy that makes the air around it shimmer.

"There," Pandit Ravi Shankar breathes, pointing to a hollow near the base of the trunk. "The charm should be hidden inside."

As they approach, the whispers rise to a fevered pitch. The ground beneath their feet begins to tremble, and a cold wind whips through the clearing, carrying with it the stench of rotting flesh.

Priya's vision swims, dark spots dancing before her eyes. She sways on her feet, feeling as if she might pass out at any moment. "Pandit-ji," she gasps. "I don't know if I can—"

Her words are cut off by a bone-chilling shriek. The air in front of the sacred tree ripples and tears, revealing a figure that makes Priya's blood run cold.

It's the sorceress, or what's left of her. Her form flickers and shifts, sometimes appearing as a beautiful woman, other times as a desiccated corpse. Her eyes burn with an unholy fire as she fixes her gaze on Priya and the priest.

"You dare to challenge me?" the spirit hisses, her voice like nails on a chalkboard. "Foolish mortals. You have no idea of the power you face."

Pandit Ravi Shankar steps forward, his voice steady despite the fear Priya can see in his eyes. "We come seeking the charm," he declares. "By the power of the ancient rites, I command you to let us pass."

The sorceress throws back her head and laughs, the sound sending shivers down Priya's spine. "Your pitiful rituals have no power here, old man. This realm is mine!"

With a gesture of her spectral hand, she sends a blast of energy towards them. Pandit Ravi Shankar barely has time to shout a protective mantra before they're both thrown backward, landing hard on the forest floor.

Priya struggles to her feet, her entire body aching. The world spins around her, and for a moment, she's not sure what's real and what's illusion. She sees her grandmother's face, contorted in agony. She hears the screams of the villagers, begging for help.

"No," she whispers, clenching her fists. "This isn't real. I won't let you win."

Drawing on a strength she didn't know she possessed, Priya pushes through the veil of confusion. She sees Pandit Ravi Shankar chanting furiously, a shimmering barrier of energy forming around them.

The sorceress howls in rage, hurling bolt after bolt of dark energy at the barrier. Each impact sends tremors through Priya's body, but she grits her teeth and stands her ground.

"The charm," the priest gasps between incantations. "You must get the charm!"

Priya nods, her eyes fixed on the hollow in the sacred tree. It's only a few meters away, but it might as well be miles with the furious spirit blocking their path.

Taking a deep breath, she waits for a break in the spirit's assault. The moment the sorceress pauses, gathering her strength for another attack, Priya makes her move.

She darts forward, her feet barely touching the ground as she races towards the tree. The sorceress shrieks in fury, redirecting her assault. Priya can feel the heat of the dark energy as it sizzles past her, singing her hair and clothes.

Just as she reaches the hollow, a tendril of shadow wraps around her ankle. Priya cries out as she's yanked backward, her fingers scrabbling at the rough bark of the tree.

"You cannot escape me," the sorceress hisses, her face inches from Priya's. "Your soul will join the others I've claimed."

Priya can feel the spirit's icy breath on her face, can see the swirling vortex of tormented souls trapped within her spectral form. For a moment, she's paralyzed with terror.

But then, through the maelstrom of fear and confusion, she hears a voice. Soft, but clear as a bell. Her grandmother's voice.

"Be strong, my child," Asha whispers. "You have the power to overcome this."

Something shifts inside Priya. The fog of fear dissipates, replaced by a clarity she's never experienced before. She locks eyes with the sorceress, no longer cowering.

"No," she says, her voice steady and strong. "You have no power over me."

With a surge of effort, Priya breaks free from the shadow's grasp. She lunges forward, plunging her arm into the hollow of the sacred tree. Her fingers close around something cool and metallic.

The moment she touches the charm, a pulse of energy radiates outward. The sorceress recoils, shrieking in pain and fury. Priya pulls the talisman from its hiding place, holding it aloft.

It's beautiful and terrifying all at once – an intricate web of silver and gold, adorned with symbols Priya doesn't recognize. As she clutches it to her chest, she feels a warmth spreading through her body, driving back the chill of fear and doubt.

"No!" the sorceress wails, her form beginning to unravel. "This cannot be!"

Pandit Ravi Shankar's voice rises in a triumphant chant. The barrier around him pulses with renewed energy, expanding outward. As it touches the spirit, she lets out an unearthly scream.

For a moment, the clearing is bathed in blinding light. Priya shields her eyes, the charm pulsing against her chest. When the light fades, the sorceress is gone. The oppressive atmosphere lifts, leaving behind a sense of peace Priya had almost forgotten.

She sags to her knees, exhausted but exhilarated. Pandit Ravi Shankar hurries to her side, his eyes wide with wonder as he gazes at the charm.

"You did it," he breathes. "Priya, you actually did it."

She manages a weak smile, her fingers tracing the intricate patterns of the talisman. "We did it," she corrects him. "But... is it over? Have we broken the curse?"

The priest's expression sobers. "Not yet," he says. "But this charm will protect you from the worst of the spirit's influence. It gives us a fighting chance."

Priya nods, struggling to her feet. As the adrenaline fades, she becomes aware of every ache and pain in her body. But there's a new strength there too, a resilience she never knew she possessed.

"Then let's get back," she says, determination glinting in her eyes. "Nani needs us. The whole village needs us."

As they make their way back through the forest, the shadows no longer seem quite so menacing. The whispers have faded, replaced by the natural sounds of the night. Priya clutches the charm close, drawing comfort from its steady warmth.

They've won a significant victory, but she knows the battle is far from over. The full moon is still approaching, and with it, the peak of the curse's power. But for the first time since this nightmare began, Priya feels a flicker of real hope.

Whatever challenges lie ahead, she's ready to face them. For her grandmother, for the village, and for herself.

7 The Healing Storm

Priya's world has narrowed to a haze of fever and pain. She tosses restlessly in her bed, tangled sheets damp with sweat. Nightmarish visions swim before her eyes - writhing shadows and grasping spectral hands. A woman's face, beautiful and terrible, looms over her. Dark eyes burn with hatred as skeletal fingers reach for Priya's throat.

She jerks awake with a strangled gasp, heart pounding. For a moment, reality blurs with her fevered dreams. Then a cool hand presses against her forehead, and her grandmother's worried face swims into focus.

"Shh, child," Asha murmurs. "You're burning up."

Priya tries to speak, but her throat is parched. She manages a weak croak. Asha holds a cup of water to her lips, supporting Priya's head as she sips. The water soothes her raw throat, but does little to ease the bone-deep ache suffusing her body.

"How long?" Priya rasps when she can speak again.

Asha's brow furrows. "Three days now. The fever won't break."

Priya closes her eyes, fighting a wave of despair. Three days lost to delirium. She can feel the curse tightening its grip, sapping her strength. How much longer can she hold out?

A distant rumble of thunder makes the windows rattle. Priya forces her eyes open, alarmed. "What was that?"

Asha's lips press into a thin line. "The storms have been getting worse. Half the village is flooded already."

As if in response, a howling gust of wind batters the house. Priya struggles to sit up, ignoring the protest of her aching muscles. "We have to do something," she insists. "The whole village is in danger."

"You're in no condition to go anywhere," Asha says firmly, easing Priya back down. "Rest. Pandit Ravi Shankar is working on a solution."

Priya wants to argue, but exhaustion drags at her. Her eyelids grow heavy. As she drifts off, she hears her grandmother murmuring a prayer.

When Priya next wakes, the room is dim. How long has she been asleep? The pounding in her head has subsided slightly, but her limbs still feel leaden. She blinks, trying to focus. A figure sits slumped in a chair by the bed. It takes Priya a moment to recognize her grandmother.

Asha looks frail, her face drawn with exhaustion. Even in sleep, worry creases her brow. With a pang, Priya realizes how much this ordeal has taken out of the older woman. Guilt twists in her gut. She's been so caught up in her own suffering, she hasn't considered the toll on her grandmother.

As if sensing Priya's gaze, Asha stirs. Her eyes flutter open, immediately seeking out her granddaughter. Relief washes over her face.

"You're awake," she says, leaning forward to brush Priya's hair back from her forehead. "How do you feel?"

"A little better," Priya lies. She doesn't want to add to her grandmother's worries.

Asha's knowing look suggests she isn't fooled. Before she can press the issue, another booming crash of thunder shakes the house. Priya flinches.

"The storm's getting closer," Asha says grimly.

Priya struggles to sit up, fighting a wave of dizziness. "We can't just wait here. There has to be something we can do."

Asha opens her mouth to reply, but is cut off by a frantic pounding at the door. She hurries to answer it, returning moments later with Pandit Ravi Shankar. The priest's usual calm demeanor is gone, replaced by grim urgency.

"It's time," he says without preamble. "We must act now, or all will be lost."

Asha nods, her jaw set with determination. "What do you need us to do?"

As Pandit Ravi Shankar outlines his plan, Priya listens with growing apprehension. Confront the spirit directly? It seems impossibly dangerous. But as another peal of thunder rattles the windows, she realizes they're out of options.

"I'll do it," Priya says, pushing herself up on shaky arms. "Whatever it takes."

"No." Asha's voice is firm. "You're too weak. I'll face the spirit."

Priya starts to protest, but the look in her grandmother's eyes stops her. There's a fire there, a strength that belies Asha's frail appearance. For the first time, Priya truly sees the fierce, determined woman who raised a family single-handedly and became a pillar of the community.

"Are you certain?" Pandit Ravi Shankar asks softly. "The risk-"

"I'm certain," Asha cuts him off. "This curse has gone on long enough. I won't stand by while it destroys everything we hold dear."

The priest nods solemnly. "Then we must prepare. There's no time to waste."

What follows is a flurry of activity. Asha and Pandit Ravi Shankar gather supplies - herbs, candles, sacred ash. Priya watches helplessly from her bed, frustration gnawing at her. She should be the one doing this, not her grandmother.

"I want to help," she insists as Asha returns with an armful of supplies.

Her grandmother's expression softens. "You can help by staying safe," she says gently. "Wear the protective charm. It will shield you from the worst of the spirit's power."

Priya fingers the talisman around her neck. Its familiar weight is oddly comforting. She nods reluctantly.

As the final preparations are made, tension fills the air. Priya can feel it pressing down on her, making it hard to breathe. Or maybe that's just the fever. She shakes her head, trying to clear it.

"It's time," Pandit Ravi Shankar announces.

Asha moves to Priya's bedside, clasping her granddaughter's hand. "Whatever happens," she says softly, "know that I love you. You've brought so much joy to my life."

Priya's throat tightens. "Nani, please-"

"Shh." Asha presses a kiss to Priya's forehead. "Have faith. We'll get through this together."

With a final squeeze of Priya's hand, Asha turns away. Pandit Ravi Shankar leads the way out of the house, into the raging storm. Priya watches them go, fear and helplessness threatening to overwhelm her.

"Be safe," she whispers.

The next hour is agony for Priya. She strains to hear anything over the howling wind and crashes of thunder. Imagination runs wild, conjuring terrifying scenarios. She pictures her grandmother facing down the vengeful spirit, defenseless against its supernatural wrath.

Unable to bear it any longer, Priya forces herself out of bed. Her legs nearly buckle, but she grits her teeth and pushes through the weakness. Stumbling to the window, she peers out into the tempest.

The village is barely visible through the driving rain. Trees bend under the onslaught, branches whipping violently. In the distance, Priya sees an eerie glow. Her breath catches. The burial site.

Before she can second-guess herself, Priya is moving. She grabs a shawl, wrapping it tightly around her shoulders. The protective charm pulses warmly against her skin as she steps out into the storm.

The wind nearly knocks her off her feet. Rain lashes her face, soaking her to the skin in seconds. Priya pushes forward, one agonizing step at a time. Her body screams in protest, but she ignores it. She has to reach her grandmother.

As she nears the burial site, the air grows thick with an oppressive energy. It presses down on Priya, making each breath a struggle. The protective charm flares brightly, creating a bubble of calm around her.

Finally, she crests a small hill. The scene before her steals what little breath she has left.

A maelstrom of dark energy swirls around the burial site. At its center stands the spirit of the sorceress, more terrifying than Priya could have imagined. Her form flickers between that of a beautiful woman and a desiccated corpse. Eyes like burning coals fix on Asha, who stands before the spirit with arms outstretched.

Pandit Ravi Shankar chants nearby, his voice barely audible over the howling wind. As Priya watches, her grandmother steps forward. Asha's voice rings out, clear and strong despite the cacophony around them.

"Great spirit," she calls, "I come before you to atone for the wrongs done to you. I offer myself as sacrifice, if it will appease your anger and lift this curse from our village."

The spirit's form coalesces, focusing intently on Asha. Priya's heart leaps into her throat. She wants to run forward, to pull her grandmother to safety. But she forces herself to remain still. This is Asha's moment.

"You dare to seek my forgiveness?" the spirit hisses, voice like nails on a chalkboard. "After all that your people have done?"

"Yes," Asha says simply. "We were wrong. The injustice done to you can never be undone. But I beg you, do not punish the innocent for the sins of the past. Take me instead, if you must have vengeance."

The spirit seems to grow larger, dark energy crackling around her. "Why should I believe you? Why should I show mercy when none was shown to me?"

Asha doesn't flinch in the face of the spirit's wrath. "Because you were once a protector of this village," she says softly. "Because despite the pain inflicted on you, I believe there is still good in your heart."

For a long moment, silence falls. Even the storm seems to hold its breath. Then the spirit lets out an agonized wail that shakes the very ground beneath their feet.

"You know nothing of my pain!" she shrieks.

Tendrils of dark energy lash out, whipping towards Asha. Priya cries out in warning, but her voice is lost in the maelstrom. She stumbles forward, desperate to reach her grandmother.

But the attack never lands. The protective charm around Priya's neck blazes with light, creating a shimmering barrier. The spirit's energy dissipates against it harmlessly.

Asha stands firm, meeting the spirit's gaze without flinching. "I may not know the depths of your suffering," she says, "but I know the pain of loss. Of betrayal. Of watching helplessly as those you love are harmed."

Her voice breaks slightly, and Priya realizes her grandmother is crying. "I'm so sorry for what was done to you. You deserved justice, not condemnation. Please, let us make this right."

The spirit's form wavers, uncertainty crossing her features. "It's too late," she whispers, and for the first time, Priya hears the pain beneath the anger. "There can be no redemption for what was done."

"It's never too late," Asha insists. She takes a step forward, hand outstretched. "Let go of your anger. Find peace. Your story deserves to be told - the truth of who you really were."

As Asha speaks, Pandit Ravi Shankar's chanting grows louder. The air thrums with spiritual energy. Priya watches in awe as the necklace in the priest's hands begins to glow.

The spirit's eyes widen. She reaches towards the necklace, longing etched on her face. "My talisman," she breathes. "You found it."

Asha nods. "It was never meant to be a curse. It was your protection, wasn't it? Your connection to the village you loved."

A sob escapes the spirit. Her form flickers rapidly, settling into the appearance of a young woman. Priya gasps softly. She's beautiful, with kind eyes and a gentle smile. This is who the sorceress truly was, before anger and pain twisted her.

"I only wanted to keep them safe," the spirit whispers. "To protect them from harm. But they turned on me. Called me a witch. Killed me for the very power they once praised."

"I know," Asha says gently. "And nothing can change that past. But we can change the future. Let your story be told. Let the truth be known."

The spirit considers this for a long moment. Then, slowly, she nods. "Perhaps... perhaps it is time to let go."

As she speaks, the necklace in Pandit Ravi Shankar's hands bursts into flames. But these are not the destructive fires that have plagued the village. This is a cleansing blaze, warm and bright.

The spirit throws back her head and lets out a cry - not of anguish this time, but of release. Her form begins to dissolve, carried away on the wind. But as she fades, Priya swears she sees a smile on the spirit's face.

"Thank you," the whisper comes, barely audible. Then she is gone.

With the spirit's departure, the unnatural storm begins to subside. The howling winds die down to a gentle breeze. The rain slows to a light drizzle. And for the first time in days, a sliver of sunlight breaks through the clouds.

Priya sways on her feet, exhaustion finally catching up with her. But before she can fall, strong arms wrap around her. She looks up into her grandmother's loving face.

"It's over," Asha murmurs, pressing a kiss to Priya's forehead. "We did it."

As the first rays of sun bathe the village in golden light, Priya feels a weight lift from her shoulders. The curse is broken. They are free.

8 A New Dawn

The days following the confrontation with the spirit bring a gradual return to normalcy for the village. As the unnatural storms subside, the damage they left behind becomes fully apparent. Fields lie flooded, trees uprooted, and homes bear the scars of wind and rain. But amid the destruction, there are signs of hope and renewal.

Priya stands at the window of her grandmother's home, watching villagers work together to clear debris and begin repairs. The fever that plagued her has finally broken, leaving her weak but clear-headed. She presses a hand to the glass, longing to be out there helping.

"You should be resting," Asha's gentle admonishment comes from behind her.

Priya turns, offering a small smile. "I've rested enough, Nani. I want to help."

Asha shakes her head fondly. "Always so stubborn. You get that from me, you know."

A comfortable silence falls between them. Priya studies her grandmother, noting the new lines of exhaustion etched on her face. But there's a lightness to Asha's bearing now, as if a great burden has been lifted.

"How are you feeling?" Priya asks softly.

Asha considers the question. "Tired," she admits. "But... at peace. For the first time in a long while."

Priya nods, understanding. The confrontation with the spirit had taken a toll on all of them, but especially Asha. Her grandmother's courage still amazes her.

"What you did was incredible," Priya says. "Standing up to the spirit like that. I don't know if I could have been so brave."

Asha reaches out, cupping Priya's cheek. "You are braver than you know, child. It was your strength that gave me courage."

Before Priya can respond, a knock at the door interrupts them. Pandit Ravi Shankar enters, looking weary but satisfied.

"I hope I'm not intruding," he says.

Asha welcomes him warmly. "Not at all. How goes the cleanup?"

"Slowly but surely," the priest replies. "The village is coming together remarkably well. There's a spirit of cooperation I haven't seen in years."

Priya can't help but smile at that. Perhaps some good has come from this ordeal after all.

"I've been meaning to ask," she says, turning to Pandit Ravi Shankar. "What happened to the necklace? After it... burned."

The priest's expression grows somber. "It was consumed entirely. Nothing remains but ash." He hesitates, then adds, "Perhaps that's for the best. Its power was too great, too dangerous."

Priya nods slowly, a pang of regret tugging at her heart. The necklace had been beautiful, for all the pain it caused. A tangible link to the past, now lost forever.

As if sensing her melancholy, Asha speaks up. "Come, let's have some tea. We could all use a moment of calm."

They settle around the small kitchen table, steam rising from their cups. For a while, they sit in comfortable silence, each lost in their own thoughts. Priya wraps her hands around the warm mug, drawing comfort from its heat.

"There's something I've been meaning to show you both," Asha says suddenly. She rises, moving to a small cabinet in the corner. When she returns, she's holding a weathered manuscript.

Priya recognizes it immediately. "The village history," she murmurs.

Asha nods. "I've been going through it again, trying to understand what happened all those years ago." She opens the manuscript carefully, flipping through brittle pages. "And I found something... unexpected."

From between two pages, she withdraws a small, folded piece of paper. It looks ancient, the edges crumbling slightly as Asha unfolds it with trembling fingers.

"What is it?" Pandit Ravi Shankar leans forward, curiosity evident in his eyes.

"A hidden note," Asha says softly. "One that changes everything we thought we knew about the sorceress."

Priya's breath catches. "What does it say?"

Asha takes a deep breath, then begins to read:

"To whoever finds this, I pray it is not too late. The woman they call witch, the one they fear and revile, is no monster. She is our protector, our guardian against forces we cannot comprehend. I have seen her turn back dark spirits that would have consumed our village. I have watched her heal the sick and bring rain to parched fields. But fear and ignorance have poisoned the minds of our people. They see her power and call it evil, never understanding the sacrifices she makes for us all. I write this in secret, for I fear what they would do if they knew I defended her. But I cannot stay silent as they hunt an innocent woman. If you read this, know the truth. Remember her not as a curse, but as a blessing we were too blind to see."

As Asha's voice fades, stunned silence fills the room. Priya's mind reels, struggling to process this revelation. Everything they thought they knew about the spirit, about the curse... it was all wrong.

"All this time," Pandit Ravi Shankar says hoarsely, "we've been living with a lie."

Asha nods, her eyes brimming with unshed tears. "She was protecting us, and we condemned her for it. No wonder her spirit was so angry, so hurt."

Priya thinks back to the moment the spirit disappeared, the look of peace that had crossed her face. "She just wanted the truth to be known," she realizes aloud.

"And now it will be," Asha says firmly. She looks at Priya, determination glinting in her eyes. "That's why I'm giving this to you, child. You have a gift for words, for telling stories. I want you to write this one - the true story of the woman we wrongly called a sorceress."

Priya's eyes widen. "Me? But I... I don't know if I can do her justice."

"You can," Asha insists. "You have the compassion to understand her pain, and the wisdom to learn from our mistakes. Tell her story, Priya. Make sure she's remembered for who she truly was."

The weight of this responsibility settles on Priya's shoulders. It's daunting, but she feels a spark of excitement kindling within her. This is a story that needs to be told, not just for the spirit's sake, but for the village's as well.

"I'll do it," she says softly. "I promise."

Pandit Ravi Shankar nods approvingly. "It will not be an easy task," he warns. "Many in the village may resist hearing a truth that challenges everything they've believed. But it is necessary."

"We'll support you every step of the way," Asha adds, squeezing Priya's hand.

As they discuss the best way to approach this delicate task, Priya feels a sense of purpose settling over her. The curse may be broken, but their journey is far from over. There is healing to be done, not just of the physical damage to the village, but of the wounds left by generations of misunderstanding and fear.

Days pass, and life in the village slowly returns to normal. The floodwaters recede, revealing fields that seem more vibrant than ever. Crops that had been withering spring back to life with surprising vigor. Even the livestock, which had been sickly and agitated during the curse, now graze contentedly in the lush pastures.

Priya throws herself into her writing, spending long hours bent over her notebook. She interviews elders, pores over old records, and pieces together the true history of the woman they had feared for so long. It's challenging work, often emotionally draining, but Priya finds it deeply fulfilling.

One evening, as the sun dips low on the horizon, Asha suggests they take a walk through the village. Priya welcomes the break, stretching muscles cramped from hours of writing.

As they stroll down the main road, the changes in the village are striking. Houses that had been damaged are nearly repaired, their walls freshly whitewashed. Gardens burst with colorful blooms. Children play in the streets, their laughter a stark contrast to the fearful silence that had gripped the village just weeks ago.

"It's amazing," Priya marvels. "Everything feels so... alive."

Asha nods, a small smile playing on her lips. "Perhaps this is the blessing she always intended for us. A chance to start anew, to build something better."

They pause at the edge of the village, looking out over the fields stretching towards the distant mountains. The setting sun paints the sky in brilliant hues of orange and pink.

"You know," Asha says thoughtfully, "I've been thinking about something. About curses and blessings."

Priya turns to her grandmother, curious. "What do you mean?"

Asha's eyes are distant, focused on some point beyond the horizon. "Sometimes, what we see as a curse is just a blessing we don't understand yet. It takes time, and often pain, for us to recognize the gift we've been given."

She looks at Priya, love and pride shining in her eyes. "This ordeal has brought so much suffering. But look at what's grown from it. The village is united in a way I've never seen before. People are kinder, more willing to help their neighbors. And you, my dear girl, have found your calling."

Priya feels a lump forming in her throat. She hadn't thought of it that way, but her grandmother is right. Through all the fear and pain, she's discovered a strength she never knew she possessed. And a purpose that fills her with excitement for the future.

"So you see," Asha continues softly, "some curses are just misunderstood blessings. It's up to us to find the light within the darkness."

As they stand there, watching the sun sink below the mountains, Priya feels a profound sense of peace settle over her. The journey has been difficult, filled with challenges she never could have imagined. But standing here, seeing the renewed life in her village and feeling the warmth of her grandmother's love, she knows it was all worth it.

The curse is broken, but its lessons will live on. In the story Priya will write, in the changed hearts of the villagers, and in the legacy of a woman who was finally understood, far too late.

As twilight deepens into night, Priya and Asha turn back towards home. The first stars are just beginning to twinkle overhead, no longer obscured by unnatural storms. Priya takes a deep breath, savoring the clean night air.

"Thank you, Nani," she says softly.

Asha squeezes her hand. "For what, child?"

Priya smiles. "For everything. For your courage, your wisdom. For helping me find my path."

Asha's answering smile is radiant. "That's what family does, my dear. We lift each other up, even in the darkest times."

As they walk home, Priya's mind is already racing with ideas for her book. She has a story to tell, a truth to unveil. And in doing so, she'll ensure that the spirit who protected their village for so long will finally receive the recognition and gratitude she always deserved.

It won't be an easy task. There will be resistance, doubts, and difficult conversations ahead. But Priya is ready to face those challenges. With her grandmother's support and the strength she's discovered within herself, she knows she can do this.

The curse may be broken, but its echoes will resonate for generations to come. In the end, perhaps that too is a kind of blessing – a reminder of the power of truth, compassion, and the unbreakable bonds of family and community.

As Priya and Asha reach their home, a soft breeze rustles through the trees. For a moment, Priya could swear she hears a whisper on the wind – a gentle "thank you" carried on the night air. She smiles, feeling a connection to the spirit that transcends time and misunderstanding.

"You're welcome," she murmurs. "And thank you, for watching over us all this time."

With a final glance at the star-studded sky, Priya follows her grandmother inside. Tomorrow will bring new challenges, but also new opportunities. The true story of the village's guardian will be told at last, and with it, a new chapter in their history will begin.

ABOUT THE AUTHOR

Priya Sharma is a passionate storyteller from a small, picturesque village nestled at the edge of an ancient forest. Growing up surrounded by the rich history and folklore of her community, Priya developed a deep love for weaving tales that bridge the past and present. Her writing is inspired by the resilience of her people and the mysteries that linger in the shadows of her hometown.

Priya's journey as a writer began with a desire to uncover and share the untold stories of her village. With a degree in literature and a heart full of curiosity, she delved into the archives, interviewed elders, and pieced together the fragments of forgotten legends. Her debut novel, crafted with love and dedication, is a testament to her belief in the power of truth and the importance of preserving cultural heritage.

When she's not writing, Priya can be found exploring the lush forests surrounding her village, seeking inspiration from the whispers of the past. She is committed to shining a light on the hidden heroes of history and hopes that her work will inspire others to look beyond the surface and discover the extraordinary within the ordinary.

Did you love *The Cursed Necklace*? Then you should read *Twilight Betrayal*[1] by Amy!

[2]

Twilight Betrayal

In the celestial realm of Suryaloka, where the balance between light and shadow is as delicate as a whisper, Samara and Maya stand at the precipice of a truth that could shatter their world. Samara, a revered warrior with an unblemished reputation, and Maya, a relentless seeker of hidden truths, stumble upon a conspiracy that threatens the very foundations of their celestial order.

---

1. https://books2read.com/u/bwgWKa

2. https://books2read.com/u/bwgWKa

Their discovery, however, does not go unnoticed. Branded as heretics by the uncompromising Deva Raj, the leader of the Eternal Council, Samara and Maya find themselves captured and silenced. Deva Raj declares their actions a grave threat to the celestial order and enacts a ruthless plan to erase all traces of their existence, hoping to prevent their "heresy" from spreading.

But the spirit of Samara and Maya's quest cannot be easily extinguished. "Twilight Betrayal" is a gripping tale of courage, love, and the relentless pursuit of truth. As the council's drastic measures aim to bury the truth and maintain their control, the bond between Samara and Maya becomes a beacon of hope in a world where deception reigns and the light of honesty is dimmed.

Join them on an epic journey through betrayal and redemption, where the quest for truth shines brightest in the darkest of times. Will the light of truth prevail, or will the shadows of deceit consume the celestial realm?

Dive into the secrets of Suryaloka and witness the timeless struggle between light and darkness. "Twilight Betrayal" is a story of heroism, resilience, and the unyielding power of love and truth.

Discover the legacy of Samara and Maya in this captivating tale that will leave you questioning the very nature of truth and justice.

www.ingramcontent.com/pod-product-compliance
Lightning Source LLC
LaVergne TN
LVHW090125160826
845673LV00015B/1022

* 9 7 9 8 2 3 0 1 7 0 4 9 5 *